CONTENTS

THE MADMAN: HIS PARABLES AND POEMS

THE FORERUNNER : HIS PARABLES AND POEMS

BEST OF
Kahlil GIBRAN

By Kahlil Gibran

Pharos Books

ISBN: 978-93-55460-39-4
eISBN: 978-93-55460-47-9

©Publisher

Publisher: Pharos Books (P) Ltd.
Plot No.-55, Main Mother Dairy Road
Pandav Nagar, East Delhi-110092
Phone: 011-40395855, +4049916623
WhatsApp: +91 8368220032
E-mail: sales@pharosbooks.in
Website: www.pharosbooks.in
First Edition: 2022

Printed By: Sushma Book Binding House, Okhla
Industrial Area, Phase II, New Delhi-110020

Best of Kahlil Gibran
By Kahlil Gibran

THE MADMAN

HIS PARABLES AND POEMS

HOW I BECAME A MADMAN

You ask me how I became a madman. It happened thus: One day, long before many gods were born, I woke from a deep sleep and found all my masks were stolen,—the seven masks I have fashioned and worn in seven lives,—I ran maskless through the crowded streets shouting, "Thieves, thieves, the cursed thieves."

Men and women laughed at me and some ran to their houses in fear of me.

And when I reached the market place, a youth standing on a house-top cried, "He is a madman." I looked up to behold him; the sun kissed my own naked face for the first time. For the first time the sun kissed my own naked face and my soul was inflamed with love for the sun, and I wanted my masks no more. And as if in a trance I cried, "Blessed, blessed are the thieves who stole my masks."

Thus I became a madman.

And I have found both freedom and safety in my madness; the freedom of loneliness and the safety from being understood, for those who understand us enslave something in us.

But let me not be too proud of my safety. Even a Thief in a jail is safe from another thief.

GOD

In the ancient days, when the first quiver of speech came to my lips, I ascended the holy mountain and spoke unto God, saying, "Master, I am thy slave. Thy hidden will is my law and I shall obey thee for ever more."

But God made no answer, and like a mighty tempest passed away.

And after a thousand years I ascended the holy mountain and again spoke unto God, saying, "Creator, I am thy creation. Out of clay hast thou fashioned me and to thee I owe mine all."

And God made no answer, but like a thousand swift wings passed away.

And after a thousand years I climbed the holy mountain and spoke unto God again, saying, "Father, I am thy son. In pity and love thou hast given me birth, and through love and worship I shall inherit thy kingdom."

And God made no answer, and like the mist that veils the distant hills he passed away.

And after a thousand years I climbed the sacred mountain and again spoke unto God, saying, "My God, my aim and my fulfillment; I am thy yesterday and thou are my tomorrow. I am thy root in the earth and thou art my flower in the sky, and together we grow before the face of the sun."

Then God leaned over me, and in my ears whispered words of sweetness, and even as the sea that enfoldeth a brook that runneth down to her, he enfolded me.

And when I descended to the valleys and the plains God was there also.

BEST OF KAHLIL GIBRAN

MY FRIEND

My friend, I am not what I seem. Seeming is but a garment I wear—a care-woven garment that protects me from thy questionings and thee from my negligence.

The "I" in me, my friend, dwells in the house of silence, and therein it shall remain for ever more, unperceived, unapproachable.

I would not have thee believe in what I say nor trust in what I do—for my words are naught but thy own thoughts in sound and my deeds thy own hopes in action.

When thou sayest, "The wind bloweth eastward," I say, "Aye it doth blow eastward"; for I would not have thee know that my mind doth not dwell upon the wind but upon the sea.

Thou canst not understand my seafaring thoughts, nor would I have thee understand. I would be at sea alone.

When it is day with thee, my friend, it is night with me; yet even then I speak of the noontide that dances upon the hills and of the purple shadow that steals its way across the valley; for thou canst not hear the songs of my darkness nor see my wings beating against the stars—and I fain would not have thee hear or see. I would be with night alone.

When thou ascendest to thy Heaven I descend to my Hell—even then thou callest to me across the unbridgeable gulf, "My companion, my comrade," and I call back to thee, "My comrade, my companion"—for I would not have thee see my Hell. The flame would burn thy eyesight and the smoke would crowd thy nostrils. And I love my Hell too well to have thee visit it. I would be in Hell alone.

Thou lovest Truth and Beauty and Righteousness; and I for thy sake say it is well and seemly to love these things. But in my heart I laught at thy love. Yet I would not have thee see my laughter. I would laugh alone.

My friend, thou art good and cautious and wise; nay, thou art perfect—and I, too, speak with thee wisely and cautiously. And yet I am mad. But I mask my madness. I would be mad alone.

My friend, thou art not my friend, but how shall I make thee understand? My path is not thy path, yet together we walk, hand in hand.

THE SCARECROW

Once I said to a scarecrow, "You must be tired of standing in this lonely field."

And he said, "The joy of scaring is a deep and lasting one, and I never tire of it."

Said I, after a minute of thought, "It is true; for I too have known that joy."

Said he, "Only those who are stuffed with straw can know it."

Then I left him, not knowing whether he had complimented or belittled me.

A year passed, during which the scarecrow turned philosopher.

And when I passed by him again I saw two crows building a nest under his hat.

THE SLEEP-WALKERS

In the town where I was born lived a woman and her daughter, who walked in their sleep.

One night, while silence enfolded the world, the woman and her daughter, walking, yet asleep, met in their mist-veiled garden.

And the mother spoke, and she said: "At last, at last, my enemy! You by whom my youth was destroyed—who have built up your life upon the ruins of mine! Would I could kill you!"

And the daughter spoke, and she said: "O hateful woman, selfish and old! Who stand between my freer self and me! Who would have my life an echo of your own faded life! Would you were dead!"

At that moment a cock crew, and both women awoke. The mother said gently, "Is that you, darling?" And the daughter answered gently, "Yes, dear."

THE WISE DOG

One day there passed by a company of cats a wise dog.

And as he came near and saw that they were very intent and heeded him not, he stopped.

Then there arose in the midst of the company a large, grave cat and looked upon them and said, "Brethren, pray ye; and when ye have prayed again and yet again, nothing doubting, verily then it shall rain mice."

And when the dog heard this he laughed in his heart and turned from them saying, "O blind and foolish cats, has it not been written and have I not known and my fathers before me, that that which raineth for prayer and faith and supplication is not mice but bones."

THE TWO HERMITS

Upon a lonely mountain, there lived two hermits who worshipped God and loved one another.

Now these two hermits had one earthen bowl, and this was their only possession.

One day an evil spirit entered into the heart of the older hermit and he came to the younger and said, "It is long that we have lived together. The time has come for us to part. Let us divide our possessions."

Then the younger hermit was saddened and he said, "It grieves me, Brother, that thou shouldst leave me. But if thou must needs go, so be it," and he brought the earthen bowl and gave it to him saying, "We cannot divide it, Brother, let it be thine."

Then the older hermit said, "Charity I will not accept. I will take nothing but mine own. It must be divided."

And the younger one said, "If the bowl be broken, of what use would it be to thee or to me? If it be thy pleasure let us rather cast a lot."

But the older hermit said again, "I will have but justice and mine own, and I will not trust justice and mine own to vain chance. The bowl must be divided."

Then the younger hermit could reason no further and he said, "If it be indeed thy will, and if even so thou wouldst have it let us now break the bowl."

But the face of the older hermit grew exceedingly dark, and he cried, "O thou cursed coward, thou wouldst not fight."

                    BEST OF KAHLIL GIBRAN

ON GIVING AND TAKING

Once there lived a man who had a valley-full of needles. And one day the mother of Jesus came to him and said: "Friend, my son's garment is torn and I must needs mend it before he goeth to the temple. Wouldst thou not give me a needle?"

And he gave her not a needle, but he gave her a learned discourse on Giving and Taking to carry to her son before he should go to the temple.

THE SEVEN SELVES

In the stillest hour of the night, as I lay half asleep, my seven selves sat together and thus conversed in whisper:

First Self: Here, in this madman, I have dwelt all these years, with naught to do but renew his pain by day and recreate his sorrow by night. I can bear my fate no longer, and now I rebel.

Second Self: Yours is a better lot than mine, brother, for it is given to me to be this madman's joyous self. I laugh his laughter and sing his happy hours, and with thrice winged feet I dance his brighter thoughts. It is I that would rebel against my weary existence.

Third Self: And what of me, the love-ridden self, the flaming brand of wild passion and fantastic desires? It is I the love-sick self who would rebel against this madman.

Fourth Self: I, amongst you all, am the most miserable, for naught was given me but odious hatred and destructive loathing. It is I, the tempest-like self, the one born in the black caves of Hell, who would protest against serving this madman.

Fifth Self: Nay, it is I, the thinking self, the fanciful self, the self of hunger and thirst, the one doomed to wander without rest in search of unknown things and things not yet created; it is I, not you, who would rebel.

Sixth Self: And I, the working self, the pitiful labourer, who, with patient hands, and longing eyes, fashion the days into images and give the formless elements new and eternal forms—it is I, the solitary one, who would rebel against this restless madman.

Seventh Self: How strange that you all would rebel against this man, because each and every one of you has a preordained fate to fulfill. Ah! could I but be like one of you, a self with a determined lot! But I have none, I am the do-nothing self, the one who sits in the dumb, empty nowhere and nowhen, while you are busy re-creating life. Is it you or I, neighbours, who should rebel?

When the seventh self thus spake the other six selves looked with pity upon him but said nothing more; and as the night grew deeper one after the other went to sleep enfolded with a new and happy submission.

But the seventh self remained watching and gazing at nothingness, which is behind all things.

WAR

One night a feast was held in the palace, and there came a man and prostrated himself before the prince, and all the feasters looked upon him; and they saw that one of his eyes was out and that the empty socket bled. And the prince inquired of him, "What has befallen you?" And the man replied, "O prince, I am by profession a thief, and this night, because there was no moon, I went to rob the money-changer's shop, and as I climbed in through the window I made a mistake and entered the weaver's shop, and in the dark I ran into the weaver's loom and my eye was plucked out. And now, O prince, I ask for justice upon the weaver."

Then the prince sent for the weaver and he came, and it was decreed that one of his eyes should be plucked out.

"O prince," said the weaver, "the decree is just. It is right that one of my eyes be taken. And yet, alas! both are necessary to me in order that I may see the two sides of the cloth that I weave. But I have a neighbour, a cobbler, who has also two eyes, and in his trade both eyes are not necessary."

Then the prince sent for the cobbler. And he came. And they took out one of the cobbler's two eyes.

And justice was satisfied.

THE FOX

A fox looked at his shadow at sunrise and said, "I will have a camel for lunch today." And all morning he went about looking for camels. But at noon he saw his shadow again—and he said, "A mouse will do."

THE WISE KING

Once there ruled in the distant city of Wirani a king who was both mighty and wise. And he was feared for his might and loved for his wisdom.

Now, in the heart of that city was a well, whose water was cool and crystalline, from which all the inhabitants drank, even the king and his courtiers; for there was no other well.

One night when all were asleep, a witch entered the city, and poured seven drops of strange liquid into the well, and said, "From this hour he who drinks this water shall become mad."

Next morning all the inhabitants, save the king and his lord chamberlain, drank from the well and became mad, even as the witch had foretold.

And during that day the people in the narrow streets and in the market places did naught but whisper to one another, "The king is mad. Our king and his lord chamberlain have lost their reason. Surely we cannot be ruled by a mad king. We must dethrone him."

That evening the king ordered a golden goblet to be filled from the well. And when it was brought to him he drank deeply, and gave it to his lord chamberlain to drink.

And there was great rejoicing in that distant city of Wirani, because its king and its lord chamberlain had regained their reason.

                    BEST OF KAHLIL GIBRAN

AMBITION

Three men met at a tavern table. One was a weaver, another a carpenter and the third a ploughman.

Said the weaver, "I sold a fine linen shroud today for two pieces of gold. Let us have all the wine we want."

"And I," said the carpenter, "I sold my best coffin. We will have a great roast with the wine."

"I only dug a grave," said the ploughman, "but my patron paid me double. Let us have honey cakes too."

And all that evening the tavern was busy, for they called often for wine and meat and cakes. And they were merry.

And the host rubbed his hands and smiled at his wife; for his guests were spending freely.

When they left the moon was high, and they walked along the road singing and shouting together.

The host and his wife stood in the tavern door and looked after them.

"Ah!" said the wife, "these gentlemen! So freehanded and so gay! If only they could bring us such luck every day! Then our son need not be a tavern-keeper and work so hard. We could educate him, and he could become a priest."

THE NEW PLEASURE

Last night I invented a new pleasure, and as I was giving it the first trial an angel and a devil came rushing toward my house. They met at my door and fought with each other over my newly created pleasure; the one crying, "It is a sin!"–the other, "It is a virtue!"

THE OTHER LANGUAGE

Three days after I was born, as I lay in my silken cradle, gazing with astonished dismay on the new world round about me, my mother spoke to the wet-nurse, saying, "How does my child?"

And the wet-nurse answered, "He does well, Madame, I have fed him three times; and never before have I seen a babe so young yet so gay."

And I was indignant; and I cried, "It is not true, mother; for my bed is hard, and the milk I have sucked is bitter to my mouth, and the odour of the breast is foul in my nostrils, and I am most miserable."

But my mother did not understand, nor did the nurse; for the language I spoke was that of the world from which I came.

And on the twenty-first day of my life, as I was being christened, the priest said to my mother, "You should indeed by happy, Madame, that your son was born a Christian."

And I was surprised,—and I said to the priest, "Then your mother in Heaven should be unhappy, for you were not born a Christian."

But the priest too did not understand my language.

And after seven moons, one day a soothsayer looked at me, and he said to my mother, "Your son will be a statesman and a great leader of men."

But I cried out,—"That is a false prophet; for I shall be a musician, and naught but a musician shall I be."

But even at that age my language was not understood—and great was my astonishment.

And after three and thirty years, during which my mother, and the nurse, and the priest have all died, (the shadow of God be upon their spirits) the soothsayer still lives. And yesterday I met him near the gates of the temple; and while we were talking together he said, "I have always known you would become a great musician. Even in your infancy I prophesied and foretold your future."

And I believed him—for now I too have forgotten the language of that other world.

                    BEST OF KAHLIL GIBRAN

THE POMEGRANATE

Once when I was living in the heart of a pomegranate, I heard a seed saying, "Someday I shall become a tree, and the wind will sing in my branches, and the sun will dance on my leaves, and I shall be strong and beautiful through all the seasons."

Then another seed spoke and said, "When I was as young as you, I too held such views; but now that I can weigh and measure things, I see that my hopes were vain."

And a third seed spoke also, "I see in us nothing that promises so great a future."

And a fourth said, "But what a mockery our life would be, without a greater future!"

Said a fifth, "Why dispute what we shall be, when we know not even what we are."

But a sixth replied, "Whatever we are, that we shall continue to be."

And a seventh said, "I have such a clear idea how everything will be, but I cannot put it into words."

Then an eight spoke—and a ninth—and a tenth—and then many—until all were speaking, and I could distinguish nothing for the many voices.

And so I moved that very day into the heart of a quince, where the seeds are few and almost silent.

THE TWO CAGES

In my father's garden there are two cages. In one is a lion, which my father's slaves brought from the desert of Ninavah; in the other is a songless sparrow.

Every day at dawn the sparrow calls to the lion, "Good morrow to thee, brother prisoner."

THE THREE ANTS

Three ants met on the nose of a man who was asleep in the sun. And after they had saluted one another, each according to the custom of his tribe, they stood there conversing.

The first ant said, "These hills and plains are the most barren I have known. I have searched all day for a grain of some sort, and there is none to be found."

Said the second ant, "I too have found nothing, though I have visited every nook and glade. This is, I believe, what my people call the soft, moving land where nothing grows."

Then the third ant raised his head and said, "My friends, we are standing now on the nose of the Supreme Ant, the mighty and infinite Ant, whose body is so great that we cannot see it, whose shadow is so vast that we cannot trace it, whose voice is so loud that we cannot hear it; and He is omnipresent."

When the third ant spoke thus the other ants looked at each other and laughed.

At that moment the man moved and in his sleep raised his hand and scratched his nose, and the three ants were crushed.

THE GRAVE-DIGGER

Once, as I was burying one of my dead selves, the grave-digger came by and said to me, "Of all those who come here to bury, you alone I like."

Said I, "You please me exceedingly, but why do you like me?"

"Because," said he, "They come weeping and go weeping—you only come laughing and go laughing."

ON THE STEPS OF THE TEMPLE

Yestereve, on the marble steps of the Temple, I saw a woman sitting between two men. One side of her face was pale, the other was blushing.

THE BLESSED CITY

In my youth I was told that in a certain city every one lived according to the Scriptures.

And I said, "I will seek that city and the blessedness thereof." And it was far. And I made great provision for my journey. And after forty days I beheld the city and on the forty-first day I entered into it.

And lo! the whole company of the inhabitants had each but a single eye and but one hand. And I was astonished and said to myself, "Shall they of this so holy city have but one eye and one hand?"

Then I saw that they too were astonished, for they were marveling greatly at my two hands and my two eyes. And as they were speaking together I inquired of them saying, "Is this indeed the Blessed City, where each man lives according to the Scriptures?" And they said, "Yes, this is that city."

"And what," said I, "hath befallen you, and where are your right eyes and your right hands?"

And all the people were moved. And they said, "Come thou and see."

And they took me to the temple in the midst of the city. And in the temple I saw a heap of hands and eyes. All withered. Then said I, "Alas! what conqueror hath committed this cruelty upon you?"

And there went a murmur amongst them. And one of their elders stood forth and said, "This doing is of ourselves. God hath made us conquerors over the evil that was in us."

And he led me to a high altar, and all the people followed. And he showed me above the altar an inscription graven, and I read:

"If thy right eye offend thee, pluck it out and cast it from thee; for it is profitable for thee that one of thy members should perish, and not that the whole body should be cast into hell. And if thy right hand offend thee, cut it off and cast it from thee; for it is profitable for thee that one of thy members should perish, and not that thy whole body should be cast into hell."

Then I understood. And I turned about to all the people and cried, "Hath no man or woman among you two eyes or two hands?"

And they answered me saying, "No, not one. There is none whole save such as are yet too young to read the Scripture and to understand its commandment."

And when we had come out of the temple, I straightway left that Blessed City; for I was not too young, and I could read the scripture.

THE GOOD GOD AND THE EVIL GOD

The Good God and the Evil God met on the mountain top.

The Good God said, "Good day to you, brother."

The Evil God did not answer.

And the Good God said, "You are in a bad humour today."

"Yes," said the Evil God, "for of late I have been often mistaken for you, called by your name, and treated as if I were you, and it ill-pleases me."

And the Good God said, "But I too have been mistaken for you and called by your name."

The Evil God walked away cursing the stupidity of man.

DEFEAT

Defeat, my Defeat, my solitude and my aloofness;
You are dearer to me than a thousand triumphs,
And sweeter to my heart than all world-glory.

Defeat, my Defeat, my self-knowledge and my defiance,
Through you I know that I am yet young and swift of foot
And not to be trapped by withering laurels.
And in you I have found aloneness
And the joy of being shunned and scorned.

Defeat, my Defeat, my shining sword and shield,
In your eyes I have read
That to be enthroned is to be enslaved,
And to be understood is to be leveled down,
And to be grasped is but to reach one's fullness
And like a ripe fruit to fall and be consumed.

Defeat, my Defeat, my bold companion,
You shall hear my songs and my cries and my silences,
And none but you shall speak to me of the beating of wings,
And urging of seas,
And of mountains that burn in the night,
And you alone shall climb my steep and rocky soul.

Defeat, my Defeat, my deathless courage,
You and I shall laugh together with the storm,

And together we shall dig graves for all that die in us,
And we shall stand in the sun with a will,
And we shall be dangerous.

NIGHT AND THE MADMAN

"I am like thee, O, Night, dark and naked; I walk on the flaming path which is above my day-dreams, and whenever my foot touches earth a giant oak tree comes forth."

"Nay, thou art not like me, O, Madman, for thou still lookest backward to see how large a foot-print thou leavest on the sand."

"I am like thee, O, Night, silent and deep; and in the heart of my loneliness lies a Goddess in child-bed; and in him who is being born Heaven touches Hell."

"Nay, thou art not like me, O, Madman, for thou shudderest yet before pain, and the song of the abyss terrifies thee."

"I am like thee, O, Night, wild and terrible; for my ears are crowded with cries of conquered nations and sighs for forgotten lands."

"Nay, thou art not like me, O, Madman, for thou still takest thy little-self for a comrade, and with thy monster-self thou canst not be friend."

"I am like thee, O, Night, cruel and awful; for my bosom is lit by burning ships at sea, and my lips are wet with blood of slain warriors."

"Nay, thou art not like me, O, Madman; for the desire for a sister-spirit is yet upon thee, and thou has not become alone unto thyself."

"I am like thee, O, Night, joyous and glad; for he who dwells in my shadow is now drunk with virgin wine, and she who follows me is sinning mirthfully."

"Nay, thou art not like me, O, Madman, for thy soul is wrapped in the veil of seven folds and thou holdest not thy heart in thine hand."

"I am like thee, O, Night, patient and passionate; for in my breast a thousand dead lovers are buried in shrouds of withered kisses."

"Yea, Madman, art thou like me? Art thou like me? And canst thou ride the tempest as a steed, and grasp the lightning as a sword?"

"Like thee, O, Night, like thee, mighty and high, and my throne is built upon heaps of fallen Gods; and before me too pass the days to kiss the hem of my garment but never to gaze at my face."

"Art thou like me, child of my darkest heart? And dost thou think my untamed thoughts and speak my vast language?"

"Yea, we are twin brothers, O, Night; for thou revealest space and I reveal my soul."

 BEST OF KAHLIL GIBRAN

FACES

Ihave seen a face with a thousand countenances, and a face that was but a single countenance as if held in a mould.

I have seen a face whose sheen I could look through to the ugliness beneath, and a face whose sheen I had to lift to see how beautiful it was.

I have seen an old face much lined with nothing, and a smooth face in which all things were graven.

I know faces, because I look through the fabric my own eye weaves, and behold the reality beneath.

THE GREATER SEA

My soul and I went to the great sea to bathe. And when we reached the shore, we went about looking for a hidden and lonely place.

But as we walked, we saw a man sitting on a grey rock taking pinches of salt from a bag and throwing them into the sea.

"This is the pessimist," said my soul, "Let us leave this place. We cannot bathe here."

We walked on until we reached an inlet. There we saw, standing on a white rock, a man holding a bejeweled box, from which he took sugar and threw it into the sea.

"And this is the optimist," said my soul, "And he too must not see our naked bodies."

Further on we walked. And on a beach we saw a man picking up dead fish and tenderly putting them back into the water.

"And we cannot bathe before him," said my soul. "He is the humane philanthropist."

And we passed on.

Then we came where we saw a man tracing his shadow on the sand. Great waves came and erased it. But he went on tracing it again and again.

"He is the mystic," said my soul, "Let us leave him."

And we walked on, till in a quiet cover we saw a man scooping up the foam and putting it into an alabaster bowl.

BEST OF KAHLIL GIBRAN

"He is the idealist," said my soul, "Surely he must not see our nudity."

And on we walked. Suddenly we heard a voice crying, "This is the sea. This is the deep sea. This is the vast and mighty sea." And when we reached the voice it was a man whose back was turned to the sea, and at his ear he held a shell, listening to its murmur.

And my soul said, "Let us pass on. He is the realist, who turns his back on the whole he cannot grasp, and busies himself with a fragment."

So we passed on. And in a weedy place among the rocks was a man with his head buried in the sand. And I said to my soul, "We can bath here, for he cannot see us."

"Nay," said my soul, "For he is the most deadly of them all. He is the puritan."

Then a great sadness came over the face of my soul, and into her voice.

"Let us go hence," she said, "For there is no lonely, hidden place where we can bathe. I would not have this wind lift my golden hair, or bare my white bosom in this air, or let the light disclose my sacred nakedness."

Then we left that sea to seek the Greater Sea.

CRUCIFIED

I cried to men, "I would be crucified!"

And they said, "Why should your blood be upon our heads?"

And I answered, "How else shall you be exalted except by crucifying madmen?"

And they heeded and I was crucified. And the crucifixion appeased me.

And when I was hanged between earth and heaven they lifted up their heads to see me. And they were exalted, for their heads had never before been lifted.

But as they stood looking up at me one called out, "For what art thou seeking to atone?"

And another cried, "In what cause dost thou sacrifice thyself?"

And a third said, "Thinkest thou with this price to buy world glory?"

Then said a fourth, "Behold, how he smiles! Can such pain be forgiven?"

And I answered them all, and said:

"Remember only that I smiled. I do not atone—nor sacrifice—nor wish for glory; and I have nothing to forgive. I thirsted—and I besought you to give me my blood to drink. For what is there can quench a madman's thirst but his own blood? I was dumb—and I asked wounds of you for mouths. I was imprisoned in your days and nights—and I sought a door into larger days and nights.

And now I go—as others already crucified have gone. And think not we are weary of crucifixion. For we must be crucified by larger and yet larger men, between greater earths and greater heavens."

THE ASTRONOMER

In the shadow of the temple my friend and I saw a blind man sitting alone. And my friend said, "Behold the wisest man of our land."

Then I left my friend and approached the blind man and greeted him. And we conversed.

After a while I said, "Forgive my question; but since when has thou been blind?"

"From my birth," he answered.

Said I, "And what path of wisdom followest thou?"

Said he, "I am an astronomer."

Then he placed his hand upon his breast saying, "I watch all these suns and moons and stars."

THE GREAT LONGING

Here I sit between my brother the mountain and my sister the sea. We three are one in loneliness, and the love that binds us together is deep and strong and strange. Nay, it is deeper than my sister's depth and stronger than my brother's strength, and stranger than the strangeness of my madness.

Aeons upon aeons have passed since the first grey dawn made us visible to one another; and though we have seen the birth and the fullness and the death of many worlds, we are still eager and young.

We are young and eager and yet we are mateless and unvisited, and though we lie in unbroken half embrace, we are uncomforted. And what comfort is there for controlled desire and unspent passion? Whence shall come the flaming god to warm my sister's bed? And what she-torrent shall quench my brother's fire? And who is the woman that shall command my heart?

In the stillness of the night my sister murmurs in her sleep the fire-god's unknown name, and my brother calls afar upon the cool and distant goddess. But upon whom I call in my sleep I know not.

Here I sit between my brother the mountain and my sister the sea. We three are one in loneliness, and the love that binds us together is deep and strong and strange.

SAID A BLADE OF GRASS

Said a blade of grass to an autumn leaf, "You make such a noise falling! You scatter all my winter dreams."

Said the leaf indignant, "Low-born and low-dwelling! Songless, peevish thing! You live not in the upper air and you cannot tell the sound of singing."

Then the autumn leaf lay down upon the earth and slept. And when spring came she waked again—and she was a blade of grass.

And when it was autumn and her winter sleep was upon her, and above her through all the air the leaves were falling, she muttered to herself, "O these autumn leaves! They make such noise! They scatter all my winter dreams."

THE EYE

Said the Eye one day, "I see beyond these valleys a mountain veiled with blue mist. Is it not beautiful?"

The Ear listened, and after listening intently awhile, said, "But where is any mountain? I do not hear it."

Then the Hand spoke and said, "I am trying in vain to feel it or touch it, and I can find no mountain."

And the Nose said, "There is no mountain, I cannot smell it."

Then the Eye turned the other way, and they all began to talk together about the Eye's strange delusion. And they said, "Something must be the matter with the Eye."

 BEST OF KAHLIL GIBRAN

THE TWO LEARNED MEN

Once there lived in the ancient city of Afkar two learned men who hated and belittled each other's learning. For one of them denied the existence of the gods and the other was a believer.

One day the two met in the marketplace, and amidst their followers they began to dispute and to argue about the existence or the non-existence of the gods. And after hours of contention they parted.

That evening the unbeliever went to the temple and prostrated himself before the altar and prayed the gods to forgive his wayward past.

And the same hour the other learned man, he who had upheld the gods, burned his sacred books. For he had become an unbeliever.

WHEN MY SORROW WAS BORN

When my Sorrow was born I nursed it with care, and watched over it with loving tenderness.

And my Sorrow grew like all living things, strong and beautiful and full of wondrous delights.

And we loved one another, my Sorrow and I, and we loved the world about us; for Sorrow had a kindly heart and mine was kindly with Sorrow.

And when we conversed, my Sorrow and I, our days were winged and our nights were girdled with dreams; for Sorrow had an eloquent tongue, and mine was eloquent with Sorrow.

And when we sang together, my Sorrow and I, our neighbors sat at their windows and listened; for our songs were deep as the sea and our melodies were full of strange memories.

And when we walked together, my Sorrow and I, people gazed at us with gentle eyes and whispered in words of exceeding sweetness. And there were those who looked with envy upon us, for Sorrow was a noble thing and I was proud with Sorrow.

But my Sorrow died, like all living things, and alone I am left to muse and ponder.

And now when I speak my words fall heavily upon my ears.

And when I sing my songs my neighbours come not to listen.

And when I walk the streets no one looks at me.

Only in my sleep I hear voices saying in pity, "See, there lies the man whose Sorrow is dead."

AND WHEN MY JOY WAS BORN

And when my Joy was born, I held it in my arms and stood on the house-top shouting, "Come ye, my neighbours, come and see, for Joy this day is born unto me. Come and behold this gladsome thing that laugheth in the sun."

But none of my neighbours came to look upon my Joy, and great was my astonishment.

And every day for seven moons I proclaimed my Joy from the house-top—and yet no one heeded me. And my Joy and I were alone, unsought and unvisited.

Then my Joy grew pale and weary because no other heart but mine held its loveliness and no other lips kissed its lips.

Then my Joy died of isolation.

And now I only remember my dead Joy in remembering my dead Sorrow. But memory is an autumn leaf that murmurs a while in the wind and then is heard no more.

"THE PERFECT WORLD"

God of lost souls, thou who are lost amongst the gods, hear me:

Gentle Destiny that watchest over us, mad, wandering spirits, hear me:

I dwell in the midst of a perfect race, I the most imperfect.

I, a human chaos, a nebula of confused elements, I move amongst finished worlds—peoples of complete laws and pure order, whose thoughts are assorted, whose dreams are arranged, and whose visions are enrolled and registered.

Their virtues, O God, are measured, their sins are weighed, and even the countless things that pass in the dim twilight of neither sin nor virtue are recorded and catalogued.

Here days and night are divided into seasons of conduct and governed by rules of blameless accuracy.

To eat, to drink, to sleep, to cover one's nudity, and then to be weary in due time.

To work, to play, to sing, to dance, and then to lie still when the clock strikes the hour.

To think thus, to feel thus much, and then to cease thinking and feeling when a certain star rises above yonder horizon.

To rob a neighbour with a smile, to bestow gifts with a graceful wave of the hand, to praise prudently, to blame cautiously, to destroy a sound with a word, to burn a body with a breath, and then to wash the hands when the day's work is done.

To love according to an established order, to entertain one's best self in a preconceived manner, to worship the gods becomingly, to intrigue the devils artfully—and then to forget all as though memory were dead.

To fancy with a motive, to contemplate with consideration, to be happy sweetly, to suffer nobly—and then to empty the cup so that tomorrow may fill it again.

All these things, O God, are conceived with forethought, born with determination, nursed with exactness, governed by rules, directed by reason, and then slain and buried after a prescribed method. And even their silent graves that lie within the human soul are marked and numbered.

It is a perfect world, a world of consummate excellence, a world of supreme wonders, the ripest fruit in God's garden, the master-thought of the universe.

But why should I be here, O God, I a green seed of unfulfilled passion, a mad tempest that seeketh neither east nor west, a bewildered fragment from a burnt planet?

Why am I here, O God of lost souls, thou who art lost amongst the gods?

BEST OF KAHLIL GIBRAN

THE FORERUNNER

HIS PARABLES AND POEMS

THE FORERUNNER : HIS PARABLES AND POEMS

You are your own forerunner, and the towers you have builded are but the foundation of your giant-self. And that self too shall be a foundation.

And I too am my own forerunner, for the long shadow stretching before me at sunrise shall gather under my feet at the noon hour. Yet another sunrise shall lay another shadow before me, and that also shall be gathered at another noon.

Always have we been our own forerunners, and always shall we be. And all that we have gathered and shall gather shall be but seeds for fields yet unploughed. We are the fields and the ploughmen, the gatherers and the gathered.

When you were a wandering desire in the mist, I too was there a wandering desire. Then we sought one another, and out of our eagerness dreams were born. And dreams were time limitless, and dreams were space without measure.

And when you were a silent word upon life's quivering lips, I too was there, another silent word. Then life uttered us and we came down the years throbbing with memories of yesterday and with longing for tomorrow, for yesterday was death conquered and tomorrow was birth pursued.

And now we are in God's hands. You are a sun in His right hand and I an earth in His left hand. Yet you are not more, shining, than I, shone upon.

And we, sun and earth, are but the beginning of a greater sun and a greater earth. And always shall we be the beginning.

You are your own forerunner, you the stranger passing by the gate of my garden.

And I too am my own forerunner, though I sit in the shadows of my trees and seem motionless.

GOD'S FOOL

Once there came from the desert to the great city of Sharia a man who was a dreamer, and he had naught but his garment and staff.

And as he walked through the streets he gazed with awe and wonder at the temples and towers and palaces, for the city of Sharia was of surpassing beauty. And he spoke often to the passers-by, questioning them about their city – but they understood not his language, nor he their language.

At the noon hour he stopped before a vast inn. It was built of yellow marble, and people were going in and coming out unhindered.

"This must be a shrine,' he said to himself, and he too went in. But what was his surprise to find himself in a hall of great splendour and a large company of men and women seated about many tables. They were eating and drinking and listening to the musicians.

'Nay,' said the dreamer. 'This is no worshipping. It must be a feast given by the prince to the people, in celebration of a great event.'

At that moment a man, whom he took to be the slave of the prince, approached him, and bade him be seated. And he was served with meat and wine and most excellent sweets.

When he was satisfied, the dreamer rose to depart. At the door he was stopped by a large man magnificently arrayed.

'Surely this is the prince himself,' said the dreamer in his heart, and he bowed to him and thanked him.

Then the large man said in the language of the city:

'Sir, you have not paid for your dinner.' And the dreamer did not understand, and again thanked him heartily. Then the large man bethought him, and he looked more closely upon the dreamer. And he saw that he was a stranger, clad in but a poor garment, and that indeed he had not wherewith to pay for his meal. Then the large man clapped his hands and called – and there came four watchmen of the city. And they listened to the large man. Then they took the dreamer between them, and they were two on each side of him. And the dreamer noted the ceremoniousness of their dress and of their manner and he looked upon them with delight. 'These,' said he, 'are men of distinction.'

And they walked all together until they came to the House of Judgement and they entered.

The dreamer saw before him, seated upon a throne, a venerable man with flowing beard, robed majestically. And he thought he was the king. And he rejoiced to be brought before him.

Now the watchmen related to the judge, who was the venerable man, the charge against the dreamer, and the judge appointed two advocates, one to present the charge and the other to defend the stranger. And the advocates rose, the one after the other, and delivered each his argument. And the dreamer thought himself to be listening to addresses of welcome, and his heart filled with gratitude to the king and the prince for all that was done for him.

Then sentence was passed upon the dreamer, that upon a tablet about his neck his crime should be written, and that he should ride through the city on a naked horse, with a trumpeter and a drummer before him. And the sentence was carried out forthwith.

Now as the dreamer rode through the city upon the naked horse, with the trumpeter and the drummer before him, the inhabitants of the city came running forth at the sound of the noise, and when they saw him they laughed one and all, and the children ran after him in companies from street to street. And the dreamer's heart was filled with ecstasy, and his eyes shone upon them. For to him the tablet was a sign of the king's blessing and the procession was in his honour.

Now as he rode, he saw among the crowd a man who was from the desert like himself and his heart swelled with joy, and he cried out to him with a shout:

'Friend! Friend! Where are we? What city of the heart's desire is this? What race of lavish hosts, who feast the chance guest in their palaces, whose princes companion him, whose kings hangs a token upon his breast and opens to him the hospitality of a city descended from heaven?'

And he who was also of the desert replied not. He only smiled and slightly shook his head. And the procession passed on.

And the dreamer's face was uplifted and his eyes were overflowing with light.

LOVE

They say the jackal and the mole
Drink from the selfsame stream
Where the lion comes to drink.
And they say the eagle and the vulture
Dig their beaks into the same carcass,
And are at peace, one with the other,
In the presence of the dead thing.
O love, whose lordly hand
Has bridled my desires,
And raised my hunger and my thirst
To dignity and pride,
Let not the strong in me and the constant
Eat the bread or drink the wine
That tempt my weaker self.
Let me rather starve,
And let my heart parch with thirst,
And let me die and perish,
Ere I stretch my hand
To a cup you did not fill,
Or a bowl you did not bless.

THE KING-HERMIT

They told me that in a forest among the mountains lives a young man in solitude who once was a king of a vast country beyond the Two Rivers. And they also said that he, of his own will, had left his throne and the land of his glory and come to dwell in the wilderness.

And I said, "I would seek that man, and learn the secret of his heart; for he who renounces a kingdom must needs be greater than a kingdom."

On that very day I went to the forest where he dwells. And I found him sitting under a white cypress, and in his hand a reed as if it were a sceptre. And I greeted him even as I would greet a king. And he turned to me and said gently, "What would you in this forest of serenity? Seek you a lost self in the green shadows, or is it a home-coming in your twilight?"

And I answered, "I sought but you - for I fain would know that which made you leave a kingdom for a forest."

And he said, "Brief is my story, for sudden was the bursting of the bubble. It happened thus: one day as I sat at a window in my palace, my chamberlain and an envoy from a foreign land were walking in my garden. And as they approached my window, the lord chamberlain was speaking of himself and saying, 'I am like the king; I have a thirst for strong wine and a hunger for all games of chance. And like my lord the king I have storms of temper.' And the lord chamberlain and the envoy disappeared among the trees. But in a few minutes they returned, and this time the lord chamberlain was speaking of me, and he was saying, 'My lord the king is like myself - a good marksman; and like me he loves music and bathes thrice a day.'

After a moment he added, "On the eve of that day I left my palace with but my garment, for I would no longer be ruler over those who assume my vices and attribute to me their virtues."

And I said, "This is indeed a wonder, and passing strange."

And he said, "Nay, my friend, you knocked at the gate of my silences and received but a trifle. For who would not leave a kingdom for a forest where the seasons sing and dance ceaselessly? Many are those who have given their kingdom for less than solitude and the sweet fellowship of aloneness. Countless are the eagles who descend from the upper air to live with moles that they may know the secrets of the earth. There are those who renounce the kingdom of dreams that they may not seem distant from the dreamless. And those who renounce the kingdom of nakedness and cover their souls that others may not be ashamed in beholding truth uncovered and beauty unveiled. And greater yet than all of these is he who renounces the kingdom of sorrow that he may not seem proud and vainglorious."

Then rising he leaned upon his reed and said, "Go now to the great city and sit at its gate and watch all those who enter into it and those who go out. And see that you find him who, though born a king, is without kingdom; and him who though ruled in flesh rules in spirit – though neither he nor his subjects know this; and him also who but seems to rule yet is in truth slave of his own slaves."

After he had said these things he smiled on me, and there were a thousand dawns upon his lips. Then he turned and walked away into the heart of the forest.

And I returned to the city, and I sat at its gate to watch the passers-by even as he had told me. And from that day to this numberless are the kings whose shadows have passed over me and few are the subjects over whom my shadow passed.

 BEST OF KAHLIL GIBRAN

THE LION'S DAUGHTER

Four slaves stood fanning an old queen who was asleep upon her throne. And she was snoring. And upon the queen's lap a cat lay purring and gazing lazily at the slaves.

The first slave spoke, and said, "How ugly this old woman is in her sleep. See her mouth droop; and she breathes as if the devil were choking her."

Then the cat said, purring, "Not half so ugly in her sleep as you in your waking slavery."

And the second slave said, "You would think sleep would smooth her wrinkles instead of deepening them. She must be dreaming of something evil."

And the cat purred, "Would that you might sleep also and dream of your freedom."

And the third slave said, "Perhaps she is seeing the procession of all those that she has slain."

And the cat purred, "Aye, she sees the procession of your forefathers and your descendants."

And the fourth slave said, "It is all very well to talk about her, but it does not make me less weary of standing and fanning."

And the cat purred, "You shall be fanning to all eternity; for as it is on earth, so it is in heaven."

At this moment the old queen nodded in her sleep, and her crown fell to the floor.

And one of the slaves said, "That is a bad omen."

And the cat purred, "The bad omen of one is the good omen of another."

And the second slave said, "What if she should wake, and find her crown fallen! She would surely slay us."

And the cat purred, "Daily from your birth she has slain you and you know it not."

And the third slave said, "Yes, she would slay us and she would call it making a sacrifice to the gods."

And the cat purred, "Only the weak are sacrificed to the gods."

And the fourth slave silenced the others, and softly he picked up the crown and replaced it, without waking her, on the old queen's head.

And the cat purred, "Only a slave restores a crown that has fallen."

And after a while the old queen woke, and she looked about her and yawned. Then she said, "Methought I dreamed, and I saw four caterpillars chased by a scorpion around the trunk of an ancient oak tree. I like not my dream."

Then she closed her eyes and went to sleep again. And she snored. And the four slaves went on fanning her.

And the cat purred, "Fan on, fan on, stupids. You fan but the fire that consumes you."

 BEST OF KAHLIL GIBRAN

TYRANNY

Thus sings the she-dragon that guards the seven caves by the sea:

"My mate shall come riding on the waves. His thundering roar shall fill the earth with fear, and the flames of his nostrils shall set the sky afire. At the eclipse of the moon we shall be wedded, and at the eclipse of the sun I shall give birth to a Saint George, who shall slay me."

Thus sings the she-dragon that guards the seven caves by the sea.

THE SAINT

In my youth I once visited a saint in his silent grove beyond the hills; and as we were conversing upon the nature of virtue a brigand came limping wearily up the ridge. When he reached the grove he knelt down before the saint and said, "O saint, I would be comforted! My sins are heavy upon me."

And the saint replied, "My sins, too, are heavy upon me."

And the brigand said, "But I am a thief and a plunderer."

And the saint replied, "I too am a thief and a plunderer."

And the brigand said, "But I am a murderer, and the blood of many men cries in my ears."

And the saint replied, " I am a murderer, and in my ears cries the blood of many men."

And the brigand said, "I have committed countless crimes."

And the saint replied, "I too have committed crimes without number."

Then the brigand stood up and gazed at the saint, and there was a strange look in his eyes. And when he left us he went skipping down the hill.

And I turned to the saint and said, "Wherefore did you accuse yourself of uncommitted crimes? See you not this man went away no longer believing in you?"

And the saint answered, "It is true he no longer believes in me. But he went away much comforted."

At that moment we heard the brigand singing in the distance, and the echo of his song filled the valley with gladness.

THE PLUTOCRAT

In my wanderings I once saw upon an island a man-headed, iron-hoofed monster who ate of the earth and drank of the sea incessantly. And for a long while I watched him. Then I approached him and said, "Have you never enough; is your hunger never satisfied and your thirst never quenched?"

And he answered saying, "Yes, I am satisfied, nay, I am weary of eating and drinking; but I am afraid that tomorrow there will be no more earth to eat and no more sea to drink."

THE GREATER SELF

This came to pass. After the coronation of Nufsibaal King of Byblus, he retired to his bed-chamber – the very room which the three hermit-magicians of the mountains had built for him. He took off his crown and his royal raiment, and stood in the centre of the room thinking of himself, now the all-powerful ruler of Byblus.

Suddenly he turned; and he saw stepping out of the silver mirror which his mother had given him, a naked man.

The king was startled, and he cried out to the man, "What would you?"

And the naked man answered, "Naught but this: Why have they crowned you king?"

And the king answered, "Because I am the noblest man in the land."

Then the naked man said, "If you were still more noble, you would not be king."

And the king said, "Because I am the mightiest man in the land they crowned me."

And the naked man said, "If you were mightier yet, you would not be king."

Then the king said, "Because I am the wisest man they crowned me king."

And the naked man said, "If you were still wiser you would not choose to be king."

Then the king fell to the floor and wept bitterly.

The naked man looked down upon him. Then he took up the crown and with tenderness replaced it upon the king's bent head.

And the naked man, gazing lovingly upon the king, entered into the mirror.

And the king roused, and straightway he looked into the mirror. And he saw there but himself crowned.

***

WAR AND THE SMALL NATIONS

Once, high above a pasture, where a sheep and a lamb were grazing, an eagle was circling and gazing hungrily down upon the lamb. And as he was about to descend and seize his prey, another eagle appeared and hovered above the sheep and her young with the same hungry intent. Then the two rivals began to fight, filling the sky with their fierce cries.

The sheep looked up and was much astonished. She turned to the lamb and said:

"How strange, my child, that these two noble birds should attack one another. Is not the vast sky large enough for both of them? Pray, my little one, pray in your heart that God may make peace between your winged brothers."

And the lamb prayed in his heart.

CRITICS

One nightfall a man travelling on horseback towards the sea reached an inn by the roadside. He dismounted and, confident in man and night like all riders towards the sea, he tied his horse to a tree beside the door and entered into the inn.

At midnight, when all were asleep, a thief came and stole the traveller's horse.

In the morning the man awoke, and discovered that his horse was stolen. And he grieved for his horse, and that a man had found it in his heart to steal.

Then his fellow lodgers came and stood around him and began to talk.

And the first man said, "How foolish of you to tie your horse outside the stable."

And the second said, " Still more foolish, without even hobbling the horse!"

And the third man said, "It is stupid at best to travel to the sea on horseback."

And the fourth said, "Only the indolent and the slow of foot own horses."

Then the traveller was much astonished. At last he cried, "My friends, because my horse was stolen, you have hastened one and all to tell me my faults and my shortcomings. But strange, not one word of reproach have you uttered about the man who stole my horse."

                    BEST OF KAHLIL GIBRAN

POETS

Four poets were sitting around a bowl of punch that stood on a table.

Said the first poet, "Methinks I see with my third eye the fragrance of this wine hovering in space like a cloud of birds in an enchanted forest."

The second poet raised his head and said, "With my inner ear I can hear those mist-birds singing. And the melody holds my heart as the white rose imprisons the bee within her petals."

The third poet closed his eyes and stretched his arm upwards, and said, "I touch them with my hand. I feel their wings, like the breath of a sleeping fairy, brushing against my fingers."

Then the fourth poet rose and lifted up the bowl, and he said, "Alas, friends! I am too dull of sight and of hearing and of touch. I cannot see the fragrance of this wine, nor hear its song, nor feel the beating of its wings. I perceive but the wine itself. Now therefore must I drink it, that it may sharpen my senses and raise me to your blissful heights."

And putting the bowl to his lips, he drank the punch to the very last drop.

The three poets, with their mouths open, looked at him aghast, and there was a thirsty yet unlyrical hatred in their eyes.

THE WEATHER-COCK

Said the weather-cock to the wind, "How tedious and monotonous you are! Can you not blow any other way but in my face? You disturb my God-given stability."

And the wind did not answer. It only laughed in space.

                                   BEST OF KAHLIL GIBRAN

THE KING OF ARADUS

Once the elders of the city of Aradus presented themselves before the king, and besought of him a decree to forbid to men all wine and all intoxicants within their city.

And the king turned his back upon them and went out from them laughing.

Then the elders departed in dismay.

At the door of the palace they met the lord chamberlain. And the lord chamberlain observed that they were troubled, and he understood their case.

Then he said, "Pity, my friends! Had you found the king drunk, surely he would have granted you your petition."

OUT OF MY DEEPER HEART

Out of my deeper heart a bird rose and flew skywards.

Higher and higher did it rise, yet larger and larger did it grow.

At first it was but like a swallow, then a lark, then an eagle, then as vast as a spring cloud, and then it filled the starry heavens.

Out of my heart a bird flew skywards. And it waxed larger as it flew. Yet it left not my heart.

O my faith, my untamed knowledge, how shall I fly to your height and see with you man's larger self pencilled upon the sky?

How shall I turn this sea within me into mist, and move with you in space immeasurable?

How can a prisoner within the temple behold its golden domes?

How shall the heart of a fruit be stretched to envelop the fruit also?

O my faith, I am in chains behind these bars of silver and ebony, and I cannot fly with you.

Yet out of my heart you rise skyward, and it is my heart that holds you, and I shall be content.

DYNASTIES

The queen of Ishana was in travail of childbirth; and the king and the mighty men of his court were waiting in breathless anxiety in the great hall of the Winged Bulls.

At eventide there came suddenly a messenger in haste and prostrated himself before the king, and said, "I bring glad tidings unto my lord the king, and unto the kingdom and the slaves of the king. Mihrab the Cruel, thy life-long enemy, the king of Bethroun, is dead."

When the king and the mighty men heard this, they all rose and shouted for joy; for the powerful Mihrab, had he lived longer, had assuredly overcome Ishana and carried the inhabitants captive.

At this moment the court physician also entered the hall of Winged Bulls, and behind him came the royal midwives. And the physician prostrated himself before the king, and said, "My lord the king shall live for ever, and through countless generations shall he rule over the people of Ishana. For unto thee, O King, is born this very hour a son, who shall be thy heir."

Then indeed was the soul of the king intoxicated with joy, that in the same moment his foe was dead and the royal line was established.

Now in the city of Ishana lived a true prophet. And the prophet was young, and bold of spirit. And the king that very night ordered that the prophet should be brought before him. And when he was brought, the king said unto him, "Prophesy now, and foretell what shall be the future of my son who is this day born unto the kingdom."

And the prophet hesitated not, but said, "Hearken, O King, and I will indeed prophesy of the future of thy son that is this day born. The soul of thy enemy, even of thy enemy King Mihrab, who died yester-eve, lingered but a day upon the wind. Then it sought for itself a body to enter into. And that which it entered into was the body of thy son that is born unto thee this hour."

Then the king was enraged, and with his sword he slew the prophet.

And from that day to this, the wise men of Ishana say one to another secretly, "Is it not known, and has it not been said from of old, that Ishana is ruled by an enemy?"

                                   BEST OF KAHLIL GIBRAN

KNOWLEDGE AND HALF-KNOWLEDGE

Four frogs sat upon a log that lay floating on the edge of a river. Suddenly the log was caught by the current and swept slowly down the stream. The frogs were delighted and absorbed, for never before had they sailed.

At length the first frog spoke, and said, "This is indeed a most marvellous log. It moves as if alive. No such log was ever known before."

Then the second frog spoke, and said, "Nay, my friend, the log is like other logs, and does not move. It is the river that is walking to the sea, and carries us and the log with it."

And the third frog spoke, and said, "It is neither the log nor the river that moves. The moving is in our thinking. For without thought nothing moves."

And the three frogs began to wrangle about what was really moving. The quarrel grew hotter and louder, but they could not agree.

Then they turned to the fourth frog, who up to this time had been listening attentively but holding his peace, and they asked his opinion.

And the fourth frog said, "Each of you is right, and none of you is wrong. The moving is in the log and the water and our thinking also."

And the three frogs became very angry, for none of them was willing to admit that his was not the whole truth, and that the other two were not wholly wrong.

Then a strange thing happened. The three frogs got together and pushed the fourth frog off the log into the river.

"SAID A SHEET OF SNOW-WHITE PAPER . . ."

Said a sheet of snow-white paper, "Pure was I created, and pure will I remain for ever. I would rather be burnt and turn to white ashes than suffer darkness to touch me or the unclean to come near me."

The ink-bottle heard what the paper was saying, and it laughed in its dark heart; but it never dared to approach her. And the multicoloured pencils heard her also, and they too never came near her.

And the snow-white sheet of paper did remain pure and chaste for ever, pure and chaste – and empty.

BEST OF KAHLIL GIBRAN

THE SCHOLAR AND THE POET

Said the serpent to the lark, "Thou flyest, yet thou canst not visit the recesses of the earth where the sap of life moveth in perfect silence."

And the lark answered, "Aye, thou knowest over much, nay thou art wiser then all things wise - pity thou canst not fly."

And as if he did not hear, the serpent said, "Thou canst not see the secrets of the deep, nor move among the treasures of the hidden empire. It was but yesterday I lay in a cave of rubies. It is like the heart of a ripe pomegranate, and the faintest ray of light turns into a flame-rose. Who but me can behold such marvels?"

And the lark said, "None, none but thee can lie among the crystal memories of the cycles - pity thou canst not sing."

And the serpent said, "I know a plant whose root descends to the bowels of the earth, and he who eats of that root becomes fairer than Ashtarte."

And the lark said, "No one, no one but thee could inveil the magic thought of the earth - pity thou canst not fly."

And the serpent said, "There is a purple stream that runneth under a mountain, and he who drinketh of it shall become immortal even as the gods. Surely no bird or beast can discover that purple stream."

And the lark answered, "If thou willest thou canst become deathless even as the gods - pity thou canst not sing."

And the serpent said, "I know a buried temple, which I visit once a moon. It was built by a forgotten race of giants, and upon its walls are graven the secrets of time and space, and he who reads them shall understand that which passeth all understanding."

And the lark said, "Verily, if thou so desirest thou canst encircle with thy pliant body all knowledge of time and space – pity thou canst not fly."

Then the serpent was disgusted, and as he turned and entered into his hole he muttered, "Empty-headed songster!"

And the lark flew away singing, "Pity thou canst not sing. Pity, pity, my wise one, thou canst not fly."

BEST OF KAHLIL GIBRAN

VALUES

Once a man unearthed in his field a marble statue of great beauty. And he took it to a collector who loved all beautiful things and offered it to him for sale, and the collector bought it for a large price. And they parted.

And as the man walked home with his money he thought, and he said to himself, "How much life this money means! How can anyone give all this for a dead carved stone buried and undreamed of in the earth for a thousand years?"

And now the collector was looking at his statue, and he was thinking, and he said to himself, "What beauty! What life! The dream of what a soul! - and fresh with the sweet sleep of a thousand years. How can anyone give all this for money, dead and dreamless?"

OTHER SEAS

A fish said to another fish, "Above this sea of ours there is another sea, with creatures swimming in it – and they live there even as we live here."

The fish replied, "Pure fancy! Pure fancy! When you know that everything that leaves our sea by even an inch, and stays out of it, dies. What proof have you of other lives in other seas?"

REPENTANCE

On a moonless night a man entered into his neighbour's garden and stole the largest melon he could find and brought it home.

He opened it and found it still unripe.

Then behold a marvel!

The man's conscience woke and smote him with remorse; and he repented having stolen the melon.

THE DYING MAN AND THE VULTURE

Wait, wait yet awhile, my eager friend.
I shall yield but too soon this wasted thing,
Whose agony overwrought and useless
Exhausts your patience.
I would not have your honest hunger
Wait upon these moments:
But this chain, though made of breath,
Is hard to break.
And the will to die,
Stronger than all things strong,
Is stayed by a will to live
Feebler than all things feeble.
Forgive me, comrade; I tarry too long.
It is memory that holds my spirit;
A procession of distant days,
A vision of youth spent in a dream,
A face that bids my eyelids not to sleep,
A voice that lingers in my ears,
A hand that touches my hand.
Forgive me that you have waited too long.
It is over now, and all is faded:
The face, the voice, the hand and the mist that brought them hither.
The knot is untied.
The cord is cleaved.
And that which is neither food nor drink is withdrawn.

Approach, my hungry comrade;
The board is made ready.
And the fare, frugal and spare,
Is given with love.
Come, and dig your beak here, into the left side,
And tear out of its cage this smaller bird,
Whose wings can beat no more:
I would have it soar with you into the sky.
Come now, my friend, I am your host tonight,
And you my welcome guest.

BEYOND MY SOLITUDE

Beyond my solitude is another solitude, and to him who dwells therein my aloneness is a crowded market-place and my silence a confusion of sounds.

Too young am I and too restless to seek that above-solitude. The voices of yonder valley still hold my ears and its shadows bar my way and I cannot go.

Beyond these hills is a grove of enchantment and to him who dwells therein my peace is but a whirlwind and my enchantment an illusion.

Too young am I and too riotous to seek that sacred grove. The taste of blood is clinging in my mouth, and the bow and the arrows of my fathers yet linger in my hand and I cannot go.

Beyond this burdened self lives my freer self; and to him my dreams are a battle fought in twilight and my desires the rattling of bones.

Too young am I and too outraged to be my freer self.

And how shall I become my freer self unless I slay my burdened selves, or unless all men become free?

How shall the eagle in me soar against the sun until my fledglings leave the nest which I with my own beak have built for them?

                    BEST OF KAHLIL GIBRAN

THE LAST WATCH

At high tide of night, when the first breath of dawn came upon the wind, the forerunner, he who calls himself echo to a voice yet unheard, left his bed-chamber and ascended to the roof of his house. Long he stood and looked down upon the slumbering city. Then he raised his head, and even as if the sleepless spirits of all those asleep had gathered around him, he opened his lips and spoke, and he said:

"My friends and neighbours and you who daily pass my gate, I would speak to you in your sleep, and in the valley of your dreams I would walk naked and unrestrained; for heedless are your waking hours and deaf are your sound-burdened ears.

"Long did I love you and overmuch.

"I love the one among you as though he were all, and all as if you were one. And in the spring of my heart I sang in your gardens, and in the summer of my heart I watched at your threshing-floors.

"Yea, I loved you all, the giant and the pygmy, the leper and the anointed, and him who gropes in the dark even as him who dances his days upon the mountains.

"You, the strong, have I loved, though the marks of your iron hoofs are yet upon my flesh; and you the weak, though you have drained my faith and wasted my patience.

"You the rich have I loved, while bitter was your honey to my mouth; and you the poor, though you knew my empty-handed shame.

"You the poet with the bowed lute and blind fingers, you have I loved in self-indulgence; and you the scholar ever gathering rotted shrouds in potters' fields.

"You the priest I have loved, who sit in the silences of yesterday questioning the fate of my tomorrow; and you the worshippers of gods the images of your own desires.

"You the thirsting woman whose cup is ever full, I have loved in understanding; and you the woman of restless nights, you too I have loved in pity.

"You the talkative have I loved, saying, 'Life hath much to say'; and you the dumb have I loved, whispering to myself, 'Says he not in silence that which I fain would hear in words?'

"And you the judge and the critic, I have loved also; yet when you have seen me crucified, you said, 'He bleeds rhythmically, and the pattern his blood makes upon his white skin is beautiful to behold.'

"Yea, I have loved you all, the young and the old, the trembling reed and the oak.

"But, alas, it was the over-abundance of my heart that turned you from me. You would drink love from a cup, but not from a surging river. You would hear love's faint murmur, but when love shouts you would muffle your ears.

"And because I have loved you all you have said, 'Too soft and yielding is his heart, and too undiscerning is his path. It is the love of a needy one, who picks crumbs even as he sits at kingly feasts. And it is the love of a weakling, for the strong loves only the strong.'

"And because I have loved you overmuch you have said, 'It is but the love of a blind man who knows not the beauty of one nor the ugliness of another. And it is the love of the tasteless who drinks vinegar even as wine. And it is the love of the impertinent and the overweening, for what stranger could be our mother and father and sister and brother?'

"This you have said, and more. For often in the market-place you pointed your fingers at me and said mockingly, 'There goes the ageless one, the man without seasons, who at the noon hour plays games with our children and at eventide sits with our elders and assumes wisdom and understanding.'

"And I said, 'I will love them more. Aye, even more. I will hide my love with seeming to hate, and disguise my tenderness as bitterness. I will wear an iron mask, and only when armed and mailed shall I seek them.'

"Then I laid a heavy hand upon your bruises, and like a tempest in the night I thundered in your ears.

"From the housetop I proclaimed you hypocrites, Pharisees, tricksters, false and empty earth-bubbles.

"The short-sighted among you I cursed for blind bats, and those too near the earth I likened to soulless moles.

"The eloquent I pronounced fork-tongued, the silent, stone-lipped, and the simple and artless I called the dead never weary of death.

"The seekers after world knowledge I condemned as offenders of the holy spirit and those who would naught but the spirit I branded as hunters of shadows who cast their nets in flat waters and catch but their own images.

"Thus with my lips have I denounced you, while my heart, bleeding within me, called you tender names.

"It was love lashed by its own self that spoke. It was pride half slain that fluttered in the dust. It was my hunger for your love that raged from the housetop, while my own love, kneeling in silence, prayed your forgiveness.

"But behold a miracle!

"It was my disguise that opened your eyes, and my seeming to hate that woke your hearts.

"And now you love me.

"You love the swords that stroke you and the arrows that crave your breast. For it comforts you to be wounded and only when you drink of your own blood can you be intoxicated.

"Like moths that seek destruction in the flame you gather daily in my garden; and with faces uplifted and eyes enchanted you watch me tear the fabric of your days. And in whispers you say the one to the other, 'He sees with the light of God. He speaks like the prophets of old. He unveils our souls and unlocks our hearts, and like the eagle that knows the way of foxes he knows our ways.'

"Aye, in truth, I know your ways, but only as an eagle knows the ways of his fledglings. And I fain would disclose my secret. Yet in my need for your nearness I feign remoteness, and in fear of the ebb tide of your love I guard the floodgates of my love."

After saying these things the forerunner covered his face with his hands and wept bitterly. For he knew in his heart that love humiliated in its nakedness is greater than love that seeks triumph in disguise; and he was ashamed.

But suddenly he raised his head, and like one waking from sleep he outstretched his arms and said, "Night is over, and we children of night must die when dawn comes leaping upon the hills; and out of our ashes a mightier love shall rise. And it shall laugh in the sun, and it shall be deathless."

           BEST OF KAHLIL GIBRAN

BOOKS PUBLISHED BY PHAROS BOOKS

 sales@pharosbooks.in  011 40395855   www.pharosbooks.in

Plot No..-55, Main Mother Dairy Road, Pandav Nagar, East Delhi-110092